ONE, two, three, four,
Mary at the cottage
door;
Five, six, seven, eight,
Eating cherries off a plate.

MY BOOK OF ENCHANTING
NURSERY RHYMES

Illustrated by Janet and Anne Grahame Johnstone

First published in Great Britain 1980 by
Deans International Publishing

This edition published in Great Britain in 1989 by
Treasure Press
Michelin House
81 Fulham Road
London SW3 6RB

Illustrations Copyright © Deans International Publishing,
a division of The Hamlyn Publishing Group Limited, 1971, 1972
This edition Copyright © Deans International Publishing,
a division of The Hamlyn Publishing Group Limited, 1980

ISBN 1 85051 410 0

A number of illustrations in this book previously appeared in
Dean's New Gift Book of Nursery Rhymes 1971,
and *Dean's Gift Book of Pussy and Puppy Nursery Rhymes* 1972.

Produced by Mandarin Offset
Printed and Bound in Hong Kong

TREASURE PRESS

O ALL you little
blackey-tops,
Pray don't eat my
father's crops,
While I lie down to
take a nap.
Shu-a-O! Shu-a-O!

LITTLE Jack Sprat
    Once had a pig;
It was not very little,
Nor yet very big.
It was not very lean,
It was not very fat—
It's a good pig to grunt,
Said little Jack Sprat.

THE Man in the moon came tumbling down,
To ask his way to Norwich.
He went by the south and burnt his mouth,
By eating cold plum-porridge.

JENNY Wren fell sick
     Upon a merry time,
In came Robin Redbreast
And brought her sops and wine.

Eat well of the sop, Jenny,
Drink well of the wine.
Thank you, Robin, kindly,
You shall be mine.

Jenny Wren got well,
And stood upon her feet;
And told Robin plainly,
She loved him not a bit.

Robin he got angry,
And hopped upon a twig,
Saying, Out upon you,
    fie upon you!
Bold faced jig!

SING a song of sixpence,
    A pocket full of rye;
Four-and-twenty blackbirds
    Baked in a pie.

When the pie was opened
    The birds began to sing;
Was not that a dainty dish
    To set before the king?

The king was in his counting-house,
Counting out his money;

The queen was in the parlour,
Eating bread and honey.

The maid was in the garden
  Hanging out the clothes;
Down came a blackbird,
  And pecked off her nose.

THE man in the wilderness asked of me,
How many strawberries grew in the sea.
I answered him,
As I thought good,
As many as red herrings
Grew in the wood.

PAT-A-CAKE, pat-a-cake, baker's man!
Make me a cake as fast as you can.
Pat it, and prick it, and mark it with T,
And put it in the oven for Tommy and me.

JACK SPRATT could eat no fat,
  His wife could eat no lean,
And so, between them both,
  They licked the platter clean.

THERE was an old woman who lived under a hill,
And if she's not gone, she's living there still.

GO to bed first,
A Golden Purse;

HERE am I, little Jumping Joan,
When I'm by myself, I'm all alone.

PLEASE to remember
  The Fifth of November,
Gunpowder treason and plot;
I see no reason
Why Gunpowder Treason
Should ever be forgot.

DAME TROT and her cat
Sat down to chat;
The Dame sat on this side
And puss sat on that.

"Puss," says the Dame,
"Can you catch a rat
Or a mouse in the dark?"
"Purr!" says the cat.

LITTLE Tommy Tucker
  Sings for his supper,
What shall we give him?
White bread and butter.
How shall he cut it
Without e'er a knife?
How shall he marry
Without e'er a wife?

"WHO goes there?"
"A Grenadier."
"What do you want?"
"A pot of beer."

MOLLY, my sister, and I fell out,
    And what do you think it was all about?
She loved coffee and I loved tea,
And that was the reason we could not agree.

O, I am His Highness's dog
from Kew,
Pray tell me, sir, whose dog
are you?

THE Robin and the Wren
Fought about the porridge-pan;
And ere the Robin got a spoon
The Wren had ate the porridge down.

HERE'S sulky Sue!
What shall we do?
Put her in the corner, till
she comes to.

I'LL sing you a song,
　Though not very long,
Yet I think it as pretty as any.
Put your hand in your purse,
You'll never be worse,
And give the poor singer a penny.

MILLIONS of massive raindrops
Have fallen all around;
They have danced on the house tops,
They have hidden in the ground.

They were liquid-like musicians,
With anything for keys,
Beating tunes upon the windows,
Keeping time upon the trees.

SIX little mice sat down to spin;
  Pussy passed by and she peeped in.
What are you doing, my little men?
Weaving coats for gentlemen.
Shall I come in and cut off your threads?
No, no, Mistress Pussy, you'd bite off our heads.
Oh, no, I'll not; I'll help you to spin.
That may be so, but you don't come in.

PUSSY CAT, pussy cat, where have you been?
I've been to London to visit the Queen!
Pussy cat, pussy cat, what did you there?
I frightened a little mouse under her chair.

PUSSY cat ate the dumplings,
  Pussy cat ate the dumplings,
Mama stood by,
And cried, Oh, fie,
Why did you eat the dumplings?

THERE was a crooked man
And he walked a crooked mile.
He found a crooked sixpence,
Against a crooked stile;
He bought a crooked cat,
Which caught a crooked mouse,
And they all lived together in a little crooked house.

AS Pussy sat on the step,
So pretty and so fair,
A neighbour's little dog came by,
Ah, Pussy, are you there?
Good morning, Mistress Pussy cat.
Come tell me how you do?
Quite well, I thank you, Puss replied;
Now tell me how are you?

LITTLE Blue Ben, who lives in the glen,
Keeps a blue cat and one blue hen,
Which lays of blue eggs a score and ten;
Where shall I find the little Blue Ben?

A cat came dancing out of a barn
    With a pair of bag-pipes under his arm.
He could sing nothing but Fiddle-cum-fee,
The mouse has married the humble-bee.
Pipe cat; dance mouse;
We'll have a wedding at our good house.

OLD Mother Shuttle
Lived in a coal-scuttle
Along with her dog and her cat.
What they ate I can't tell,
But 'tis known very well
That not one of the party was fat.

Old Mother Shuttle
Scoured out her coal-scuttle
And washed both her dog and her cat.
The cat scratched her nose,
So they came to hard blows,
And who was the gainer of that?

HIE, hie, says Anthony,
    Puss in the pantry
Gnawing, gnawing
A mutton mutton-bone.
See how she tumbles it,
See how she mumbles it,
See how she tosses
The mutton mutton-bone.

RIDE away, ride away
    Johnny shall ride,
He shall have a pussy cat
Tied to one side;
He shall have a little dog
Tied to the other,
And Johnny shall ride
To see his grandmother.

POUSSIE, POUSSIE, baudrons,
Where have ye been?
I've been at London
Seein' the king!
Poussie, poussie, baudrons,
What got ye there?
I got a wee mousie,
Rinnin' up a stair!

PUSSIE sat upon the wall;
Pussie said, "Mee-ow"
And that was all.

PUSSY cat, pussy cat,
          Where have you been?
I've been to see grandmother
Over the green!
What did she give you?
Milk in a can.
What did you say for it?
Thank you, Grandam!

HEY, my kitten, my kitten,
  And hey my kitten, my deary!
Such a sweet pet as this
There is not far nor neary.
Here we go up, up, up.
Here we go down, down, downy;
Here we go backwards and forwards,
And here we go
  round, round,
    roundy.

OLD Dame Trot,
    Some cold fish had got,
Which for pussy,
She kept in Store.
When she looked there was none
The cold fish had gone,
For Puss had been there before.

I William of the Wastle
Am now in my Castle,
And awe the Dogs in the Town
Shan't gar me gang down.

HEY, diddle dout,
   My candle's out,
My little maid's not at home;
Saddle the hog, bridle the dog,
And fetch my little maid home.

THIS old man, he went one,
　　He went Nick Nack
On my drum!
Nick Nack Paddy Whack!
Give a dog a bone,
This old man came rolling home.

OLD Farmer Giles
Walked seven miles
With his faithful dog, old Rover;
And old Farmer Giles
When he came to the stiles,
Took a run, and jumped clean over.

I had a little dog, and his name was Blue Bell, I gave him some work, and he did it very well;

I sent him up stairs to pick up a pin, He stepped in the coal-scuttle up to his chin.

I sent him to the garden to pick some sage, He tumbled down and fell in a rage; I sent him to the cellar, to draw a pot of beer, He came up again and said there was none there.

HARK, hark,
    The dogs do bark,
The beggars are coming to town;
Some in rags,
And some in tags,
And one in a velvet gown.

OH where, oh where
  Has my little dog gone?
Oh where, oh where can he be?
With his ears cut short
And his tail cut long,
Oh where, oh where is he?

TELL tale tit—
    Your tongue shall be slit
And every little puppy-dog
Shall have a little bit.

HODDLEY, poddley, puddle and frogs,
  Cats are to marry the poodle dogs;
Cats in blue jackets and dogs in red hats,
What will become of the mice and the rats?

THERE was once a nice little dog Trim
    Who ne'er had ill temper or whim.
She could sit up and dance—
Could run, skip and prance—
Who would not like little dog Trim?

Hey diddle diddle the Cat and the Fiddle • The Cow jumped over the Moon • The little Dog laughed to see such fun • And the Dish ran away with the Spoon •